ALPACA

For Betty

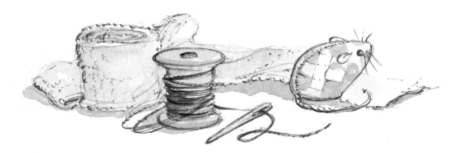

First published in Great Britain 1982 by William Collins Sons & Co Ltd
First published in Picture Lions 1984
by William Collins Sons & Co Ltd
8 Grafton Street, London W1
Copyright © Text Rosemary Billam 1982
© Illustrations Vanessa Julian-Ottie 1982
Printed in Great Britain
by William Collins Sons & Co Ltd, Glasgow

ALPACA

Rosemary Billam

Pictures by Vanessa Julian-Ottie

**FONTANA
PICTURE LIONS**

Alpaca Rabbit had been with the family for
as long as he could remember. His dungarees
were faded. He had a hole in the elbow of his
jersey, and his buttons were all odd ones of
different sizes. One of the stitches of his mouth
had come undone, and he couldn't even smile.

His little girl, Ellen, kept telling him to cheer
up. He tried, but he felt lonely and down in
the dumps.

He remembered the old days when Ellen used
to take him to school in her satchel. That was
interesting. He liked learning things. He liked
the other children.

He used to sit next to Ellen,
and help her with her sums,

and watch her painting.

But recently Ellen had started leaving
him at home with the other toys.

On her birthday, for the first time, Ellen forgot to take Alpaca downstairs for her birthday party. He could hear the children in the front room, dancing to music and playing games. He sighed. He felt a bit left out. He decided to go and have a little peek, so he climbed off the bed, and tiptoed out onto the landing.

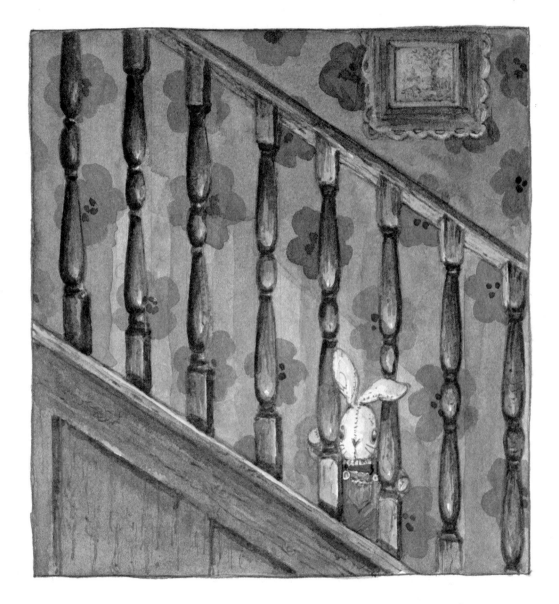

He lowered himself down the stairs, and
pushed his head between the bannister rails.

He could see Ellen opening her presents.
There were pieces of wrapping paper, and bits
of ribbon, and cards and envelopes all over
the floor. Alpaca had never seen so many
presents.
There were cries of delight as Ellen opened a
box and took out a pink doll with curly hair
and shiny black shoes.
Alpaca thought that she looked a perfectly
ordinary sort of doll.

Ellen was excitedly opening her next parcel.
Inside was a feathery owl, wearing a pair of
spectacles. Ellen showed him off to her friends.
Alpaca couldn't see what all the fuss was
about.
Ellen's mother started to light the candles on
the cake.
"I'll just shut the door so that the draught
doesn't blow them out," she said.

It was dark and cold on the landing and
Alpaca couldn't watch the party any more, so
he went back to Ellen's room and climbed up
on the bed. He kept thinking what a lot of fun
the children were having.

That night Ellen was allowed to stay up late.
When it was time for bed, she had to get out
of her party dress and into her nighty very
quickly. She put the pink doll and the owl
onto her bed next to Alpaca.

"Move up, Alpaca," she said.

Alpaca wished the new toys didn't take up so much room. He nudged the owl to make him move up a bit. The owl pecked him. Alpaca didn't think that was very polite.

Alpaca hoped that Ellen would see he was being squashed, but after saying goodnight, she went straight off to sleep because she was so tired.

"Excuse me," he whispered to the pink doll,
"but I need a bit more space." She pretended
not to hear. Alpaca gave her a push, but she
pushed him back and Alpaca fell over the side
and rolled underneath the bed.

It was very cold on the floor all night but, what was worse, nobody noticed that he was missing in the morning. He lay sadly there all day, sneezing in the dust. Nobody heard. Alpaca wondered if Ellen would remember him when she came home from school. Would she think of looking under the bed?

At four o'clock, Ellen's friend, Mary, came
round to play.
"What shall we do until tea-time?" asked
Mary.
"Let's play nurses," said Ellen.
They got out Ellen's nursing kit and uniform
from the cupboard.

The girls put all the toys into hospital, but
Ellen wasn't happy. Something wasn't right.
Something was missing.
"Where's Alpaca?" she said.
The girls searched in the wardrobe, and
behind the curtains, and under the bedcovers.

"He's got lost," said Mary.

"He must be hiding," said Ellen.

She looked under the bed.

"Alpaca! What are you doing down there?
You're all dusty."

Ellen picked Alpaca up and gave him a hug.

Ellen was surprised how thin he'd become.
"I remember when Mummy first made you.
You were so cuddly and cheerful and bright,"
she said. She looked at Alpaca and noticed
that the wool on his tummy had worn away,
and that he was losing some of his stuffing.
"Look," she whispered to Mary.
"I could take him home with me and make
him better," said Mary. "I'd swap my
kaleidoscope for him," she added.
Alpaca was suddenly very frightened. Mary
was quite a nice little girl but he didn't want
to go and live at her house. What would Ellen
say?

Ellen didn't need time to think.
She answered straight away.
"I couldn't swap Alpaca for anything. He's
always been my best friend. I can make him
better."
Alpaca felt happy through and through.

Mary took his temperature and made charts for all the other patients, while Ellen threaded a needle for the operation. She got the syringe out of her nursing kit and gave Alpaca an injection. "It won't hurt now," she told him.

Ellen pushed all his stuffing back in and
sewed him up.

"All over now!" she said.

She also put another stitch in his lips so that
he could smile again. Ellen and Alpaca smiled
at each other.

Ellen fussed over Alpaca while Mary gave the
owl some medicine, and tied a bandage round
the pink doll's arm.

"What are their names?" asked Mary.

"They haven't got names yet," said Ellen.

Alpaca looked across at the new toys, sitting
in the old cot. He thought how horrible it
must be not to have a name.
"What are you going to call them?" asked
Mary.
"I'll call the owl Wisey because he's wise and
I'll call the doll Jane because . . . she looks
like a Jane," said Ellen.
Ellen's mother called, "Tea's ready,"
so the girls ran downstairs. Alpaca
went over to Jane and Wisey.
"Hello," he said, "My name's Alpaca."

Just then, the door opened, and Ellen and
Mary came back. They sat all the toys down
in a circle, and set out the dolls' tea-service.
Mary poured the orange juice and Ellen
shared out the birthday cake. She gave Alpaca
the biggest piece because he'd been so brave.
"It's nice to have friends," thought Alpaca,
smiling.